# A Night
# to Remember

**BBC**

It was a beautiful day in the garden, but Slowcoach hadn't noticed. He was very cross about something. He grumbled and muttered so loudly that he woke up Bill and Ben.

Bill and Ben wondered what was wrong, so they zipped over to Slowcoach's house to find out.

"*Slobbadob!*" called Bill. "*Whattaslubalub?*" called Ben. Slowcoach came to his door and peered out.

"Is that you two troublemakers?" he asked. "What do you want?"

Bill and Ben said they didn't want anything. They were just wondering what Slowcoach was moaning about.

"I'll tell you," said Slowcoach.
"I was reading a very interesting book
last night when I must have nodded off.
And there they were. Gone."
"*Flob?*" asked Bill.
"My spectacles!" said Slowcoach.
"Someone had pinched my spectacles!
And I can't see a thing without them!"

Bill had an idea.
*"Flobbalob!"* he said.

He and Ben would find the glasses thief
for Slowcoach and get his spectacles back for him.
"I'll believe that when I see it," muttered Slowcoach,
and he stomped back inside.

Bill thought that, because the spectacles were stolen at night,
it was quite likely the thief would wait until darkness before
he tried to take anything else. He whispered his plan to Ben.
This time, they would be ready for him!

That night, while Weed was fast asleep between the flowerpots, Bill got up.

"*Flobbaden?*" he called, softly.
Ben was still asleep.
Bill went over to Ben's pot and looked inside. Then he whacked the side of the pot with a stick.

# Bang, bang, bang!

Ben shot out of his pot and landed in a dazed heap next to Bill. Bill reminded Ben about their plan to find the mysterious glasses thief.

*"Ah! Flub!"* said Ben, tapping the side of his nose, knowingly.

The flowerpot men crept very quietly along to the potting shed.
Suddenly, an owl hooted.

# "HOOOOOT…hoo…hoot!"

"*WAAAGGGHHH!*" yelled Ben, and jumped
into Bill's arms, terrified.

But Bill was terrified, too, and dropped him.

"WAAAAGGGHHH!"

There was only one thing to do...
"*Flobbadide!*" they said.

They hid behind a watering can and began to wonder if catching the glasses thief was such a good idea after all. Having gone this far, though, they decided they weren't going to give up.
Suddenly, they heard something else…

"Sssnnooorrre…"

"*Flobbadat?*" asked Bill, looking around. "*Flobbadistle?*"

No, Thistle was sleeping quietly.

**"Sssnnooorrre…"**
There it was again.
It was coming from the kennel!
***"Flobbanotathistle!"*** said Bill, his knees shaking.

Bravely, the flowerpot men made their way into the kennel. At last, they thought they might have found the thief.

**"Sssnnooorre ... lovelysluggysandwich..."**

*"**Flobbadoo!**"* said Bill.

He and Ben began to giggle. It was Boo!

Boo was not at all pleased to be woken up. And when they explained they were looking for a glasses thief, he said, "Well, if you think it was me … you can just think again! Now, if you don't mind, I've got some sleep to catch up on!"

And with that, he rolled himself up into a ball again.

Suddenly, the flowerpot men heard another noise...

# "Oooogh...whooogh!"

*"Flubbadat?"* said Ben.
Nervously, Bill and Ben tiptoed over to Ketchup's
greenhouse. There, they found Ketchup shivering and
moaning, blue with the cold.

"Thank goodness you've c...c...come," said Ketchup. "The man left the greenhouse door open last night and I'm fff...freezing! You couldn't close it, could you?"

Bill and Ben closed the greenhouse door for Ketchup,
and made their way back to their flowerpots.
They still hadn't found the glasses thief.
Then they heard some strange noises coming from
Slowcoach's house.
It sounded as if the thief had returned!

Quickly, they went inside.

"***Flobbadob!***" said Bill.
It was just Slowcoach
tossing, turning and
dreaming in his sleep!

Bill thought the thief might still come, so they decided to stay and watch over Slowcoach's house.

But the tired flowerpot men just couldn't stay awake…

…and they gradually fell fast asleep…

…outside Slowcoach's doorway.

The following morning, Slowcoach
pushed them out of the way. "It's
a bit early for fun and games, isn't
it?" he said, crossly. "Well?
Did you catch the thief?"

Bill and Ben looked at each other.
"*Flob*," said Bill, shaking his head.
"*Flubaleep*," said Ben.

"You fell asleep!" said Slowcoach.
"Useless pair. And talking of sleep,
I had a terrible night last night.
It was as if something was stuck
inside my shell. Just a minute…"

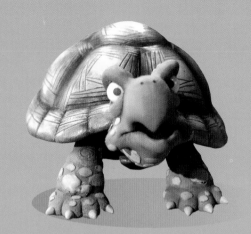

He pulled himself into his shell and
rummaged around inside for a bit.
Then he popped his head out again –
and he was wearing his spectacles!

"Well, would you believe, it!" he said. "They were in my shell all that time!" Slowcoach chuckled to himself. "Heh, heh! Most amusing."

Bill and Ben were speechless.

"Hee, hee! Oh, you poor things," said Weed.
"All that trouble for nothing!"
But the flowerpot men were too tired to
say anything. After their night of adventure,
all they wanted to do was sleep!

**The End**